OUR story so far...

WRITTEN BY _____

IN THE YEAR _____

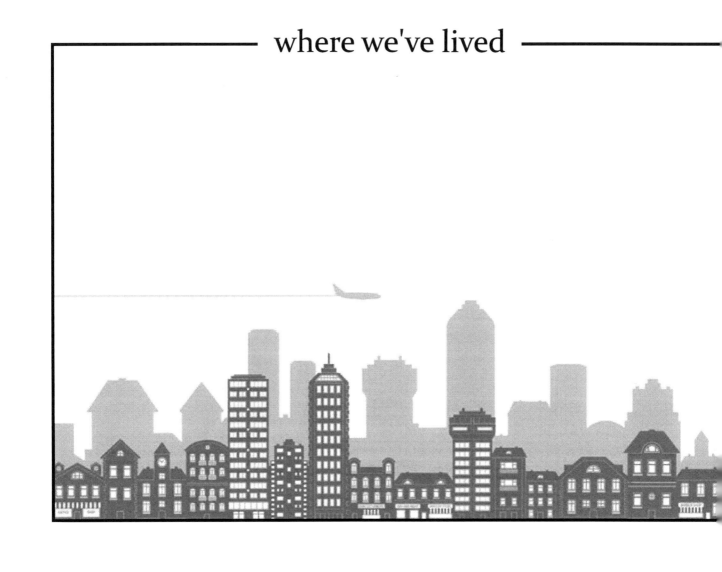

Whatever *life Throws at us*

We Will

_____

_____

_____

_____

_____

How We met

Important Milestones :

YEAR DATE :

EVENT:

our most memorable dates

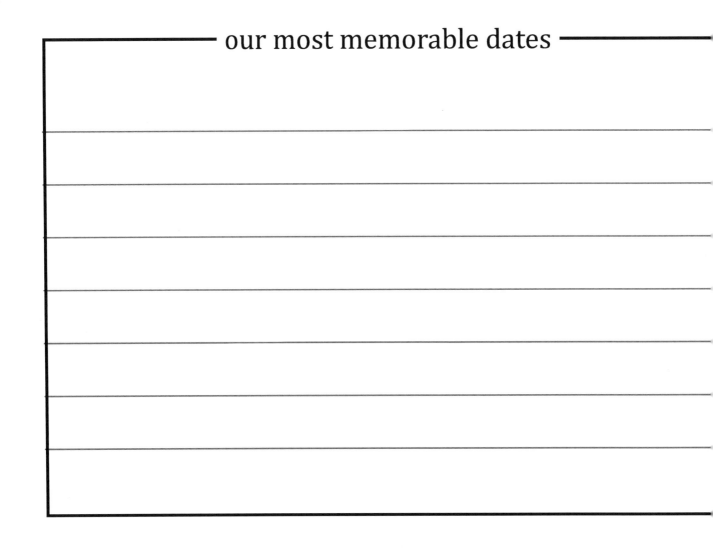

our most memorable dates

date ideas for the future

date ideas for the future

our *favourites:*

FOODS: _____

DRINKS: _____

MOVIES: _____

TV SHOWS: _____

SONGS: _____

ARTISTS/BANDS: _____

WEEKEND ACTIVITY: _____

our proudest achievements

our proudest achievements

ME *or* YOU ?

Dreams and the Future

Where is a place you've always wanted to travel? _____

What is something you want to do together that we haven't? _____

Have you ever wanted to move anywhere else? _____

If you could gain one quality or ability, what would it be? _____

How do you see the future individually and collectively as a couple? _____

What things do you look forward to each day? _____

How do you foresee us resolving our most persistent problems? _____

What are your goals for this relationship? _____

What are you hoping to learn in the coming year? _____

ME *or* YOU ?

Favorites

What is your favorite film? _____

What was your favorite class? _____

What is your favorite book? _____

What is your favorite childhood memory? _____

What is your favorite memory of our relationship? _____

What is your favorite thing about yourself? _____

What is your favorite thing about me? _____

What is your favorite place? _____

What was your favorite part about our first kiss? _____

What was your favorite date we've had? _____

ME *or* YOU ?

What is the extent of your religious ideology, if any? _____

Is there anything you would change about yourself? _____

What are some of the things that you are most grateful for? _____

When was the last time you cried? _____

What does a perfect day look like to you? _____

Do you trust me? _____

Which family member did you admire most when you were young? _____

What does a balanced relationship look like to you? _____

What is your idea of a healthy relationship? _____

Remember When?

Remember When?

Remember When?

Reasons I Love You:

Reasons I Love You:

_____

_____

_____

_____

_____

_____

Reasons I Love You:

_____

_____

_____

_____

_____

_____

Reasons I Love You:

_____

_____

_____

_____

_____

_____

Thank You
for:

_____

_____

_____

_____

_____

Thank You
for:

_____

_____

_____

_____

_____

_____

Thank You
for:

_____

_____

_____

_____

_____

_____

Made in the USA
Monee, IL
24 January 2022